忠犬八公

Hachiko: The True Story of a Loyal Dog

[美] 帕梅拉·S. 特纳（Pamela S. Turner）——著

[法] 扬·纳欣贝内（Yan Nascimbene）——绘　尹楠———译

湖南文艺出版社
HUNAN LITERATURE AND ART PUBLISHING HOUSE

小博集

著作权合同登记号:图字18-2021-48

图书在版编目(CIP)数据

忠犬八公:汉、英 / (美)帕梅拉·S.特纳
(Pamela S. Turner)著;(法)扬·纳欣贝内
(Yan Nascimbene)绘;尹楠译. -- 长沙:湖南文艺出版社,2021.9
书名原文:HACHIKO: The True Story Of A Loyal
Dog
ISBN 978-7-5726-0239-9

Ⅰ.①忠… Ⅱ.①帕… ②扬… ③尹… Ⅲ.①长篇小说-美国-现代-汉、英 Ⅳ.①I561.45

中国版本图书馆CIP数据核字(2021)第140238号

上架建议:儿童文学

ZHONGQUAN BAGONG: HAN、YING

忠犬八公:汉、英

作　　者:〔美〕帕梅拉·S.特纳(Pamela S. Turner)
绘　　者:〔法〕扬·纳欣贝内(Yan Nascimbene)
译　　者:尹　楠
出 版 人:曾赛丰
责任编辑:吕苗莉
策划编辑:文赛峰　李柯慧　马　瑄
特约编辑:张丽霞
营销支持:付　佳　付聪颖　周　然
版权支持:张雪珂
封面设计:霍雨佳
版式设计:霍雨佳
出　　版:湖南文艺出版社
　　　　　(长沙市雨花区东二环一段508号　邮编:410014)
网　　址:www.hnwy.net
印　　刷:北京尚唐印刷包装有限公司
经　　销:新华书店
开　　本:889 mm×1194 mm　1/32
字　　数:20千字
印　　张:2.25
版　　次:2021年9月第1版
印　　次:2021年9月第1次印刷
书　　号:ISBN 978-7-5726-0239-9
定　　价:35.00元

若有质量问题,请致电质量监督电话:010-59096394　团购电话:010-59320018

★ 序

试着想象一下，想象每天走到同一个地方去见你最好的朋友，想象每天早晨和下午看着成百上千人从你身旁经过，想象你一直在等待、等待、等待，等待了十年。这就是八公所做的事情。

八公是一只真实存在过的狗狗，生活在东京，在它的主人离开它之后的漫长岁月中，它仍然忠实地守候在涩谷火车站，等待主人的出现。它的忠诚远近闻名，每天经过这个火车站的人都对它崇拜有加。这就是小男孩健太郎眼中的忠犬八公的故事，他和这只特别的狗狗之间的友谊永远地改变了他的生活。

本书内容简单易懂，同时配有法国知名插画师扬·纳欣贝内漂亮的水彩插图。忠犬八公的传奇故事打动了全世界无数人，它也将触动你的心扉，给予你无穷的力量。

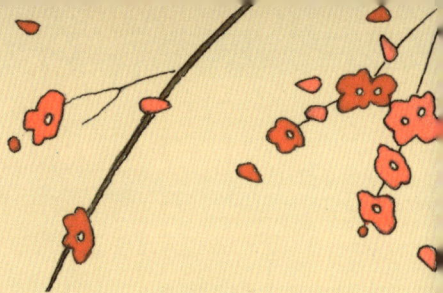

忠犬八公

　　涩谷火车站门口有我老朋友的雕像，它那青铜铸就的脚已经被无数善意的抚摸擦得锃亮。雕像下方有一块牌子，上面简单地写着"忠犬八公"。我闭上眼睛，想起我们相遇的那一天。那已经是很久以前的事了。

在我六岁的时候，全家搬到了东京涩谷火车站附近的一套小房子里生活。一开始，来来往往的火车把我吓坏了。但过了一段时间，我开始享受火车经过时的震颤和它们发出的热闹的声响。一天下午，我央求妈妈带我一起去迎接乘坐火车回家的爸爸。妈妈笑着说："健太郎，你已经长大了，变勇敢了，像个武士了！"然后我们一起向火车站走去。

当时正值春天，天气晴朗而寒冷。火车站周围到处都是商贩们的手推车，他们正向行色匆匆的路人叫卖着零食、报纸和其他东西。身着和服的女士们走得小心翼翼，唯恐自己的厚底短袜沾上路上的灰尘。商人们则大步向前，急匆匆的，要么赶着回家，要么赶着去搭另一趟火车。我和妈妈在火车站门口停了下来，就在这时，我注意到了那只狗。

它独自安静地坐在一个报摊旁，一身奶油色的毛紧密厚实，耳朵又小又尖，身后还有一条毛茸茸的大尾巴，弯弯地翘在了背上。我怀疑它是一条流浪狗，但它戴着漂亮的皮背带，看起来很健康、很强壮。

它那双棕色的眼睛牢牢盯着火车站的入口。

就在这时，爸爸出现了。他正在和一位年长的男人聊天。那只狗向那人扑过去，整个身体高兴地扭动起来。它的眼睛闪闪发光，嘴角翘起，在我看来像是在微笑。

"啊，健太郎！你瞧，上野博士，你不是唯一一个有人来接的人。"爸爸说道。他把我们介绍给那位长者。"上野博士跟我一样在东京帝国大学工作。"

"您的狗叫什么名字？"我害羞地问道。那只狗很漂亮，但它棱角分明的脸让我想起狼的样子。我抓紧妈妈的和服，躲到她身后，以防万一。

"别害怕，"上野博士亲切地说道，"这是八公。它个头很大，但还是只小狗。它每天早上送我到火车站，下午又到这儿来等我回家。我想八公是把一整天的快乐都存了起来，然后在瞬间释放出来！"

八公在上野博士身旁摇着尾巴。我伸出手去摸它，它就跳上前来使劲闻我的脸。我大叫一声，跳回妈妈身后。

他们都大笑起来。"哦，健太郎，别担心——它只是想认识你。"上野博士说道，"狗只需要闻一闻，就能知道很多关于人的信息。哎呀，八公可能知道了你午餐吃了什么！"

我闻了闻我的手，但闻起来并不像饭团的味道啊。我伸出手，轻轻地拍了拍八公的肩。"它的毛很厚，很软，"我说道，"好像一只熊。"

　　"在北方，像八公这样的狗曾经可以猎捕熊呢，那里寒冷而多雪。"上野博士一边说，一边在我身旁蹲了下去，抚摸八公的耳朵。

从那天起，我几乎每天下午都去火车站。但我不再去看火车，我去看八公。它总是在那儿，就在报摊附近等待。我经常从午餐中省下一点点吃的，藏在我的一个口袋里。八公就摇着尾巴，把我闻一遍，直到从我身上找到一小块黏糊糊的鱼肉或豆饼，然后它就用鼻子轻轻推我一下，好像在说："给我奖励！"天冷的时候，我就把脸埋进它脖子上厚厚的奶油色毛圈里。

五月的一天，我和八公一起在火车站等着。我一看到爸爸，就知道出事了。只有他一个人。他佝偻着身子走着，眼睛盯着脚下灰色的人行道，神情悲伤。

"怎么了，爸爸？"我一只手放在八公的大脑袋上，焦急地问道。爸爸叹了口气，说："健太郎，我们回家吧。"我们离开的时候，八公那双明亮的棕色眼睛一直盯着我们，但它留了下来，继续等待上野博士。

回到家，爸爸告诉我们，上野博士当天早上在大学去世了。我惊呆了。"八公怎么办？"我问道，使劲眨眼睛，强忍住泪水，"它会做什么？"

"我不知道，"爸爸答道，"也许上野博士的亲戚会把它带走。"

　　"那今天晚上呢？"我问道，"不知道它怎么样了，我们能去看看它吗？"

爸爸很伤心，也很疲惫，但他还是陪我回到了涩谷火车站。八公蜷缩在报摊旁。它一看见我们就摇起尾巴来。我和爸爸用一个破碗给它盛了一点水和一些吃的。八公开始吃饭、喝水，但它总是抬头看向火车站的入口，寻找上野博士的身影。我和爸爸离开的时候比我们来的时候还要伤心。

第二天，我回去看八公，但它不在那儿。爸爸告诉我，八公被带到了几英里外，跟上野博士的亲戚住在一起。"可是那样我就再也见不到它了！"我哭着说道，"它为什么不能和我们住在一起？"

"我们家没地方养狗，"爸爸解释道，"而且现在上野博士去世了，八公的确应该属于他的亲戚。八公有个家，总好过守在火车站。"

但是八公另有想法。几天后，它回到了涩谷火车站，棕色的眼睛盯着火车站的入口，耐心地等待着。八公先是跑回了旧家，然后又从那儿跑到了涩谷火车站。

妈妈和爸爸让我每天给八公送去食物和水。虽然妈妈对送吃的有点抱怨，说我们养不起熊一样的八公，但她做的米饭似乎总是比我们所能吃下的要多。

火车站的其他人也注意到了八公。跟爸爸和上野博士一起坐火车的男男女女都会停下来挠挠八公的耳朵，对它说几句好话。一天，我看到一位老爷爷给八公的水盆加水时，八公在不停地舔他的手。这位老爷爷头发花白，佝偻着腰，仿佛一生中大部分时间腰都直不起来。但他的眼睛和八公的眼睛一样炯炯有神。

　　"你是健太郎吗？"老爷爷问我。我点点头。"我是小林。我是上野博士的园丁。

　　"上野博士跟我说过，你和八公常常一起等待下午的火车。"

"您还在照看上野博士的房子吗？"我问道。

"是的，"小林先生答道，"八公每天晚上都会回来，睡在门廊上。但是到了早上，它就走去火车站，就像从前送上野博士去火车站一样。最后一班火车离站后，它才回家。"

我们都沉默了。过了一会儿，我问道："您觉得八公知道上野博士死了吗？"

小林先生若有所思地说道："我不知道，健太郎。也许它仍然希望上野博士有一天会回来。也许它知道上野博士已经死了，但它还是守在火车站，怀念着它的主人。"

随着时光流逝，八公渐渐老去，变得四肢僵硬，几乎没法走到涩谷火车站。但它还是每天都去。人们开始筹款，想在火车站为八公建一座雕像。爸爸、妈妈和我都捐了钱，当雕像被放置在八公等候多年的地方旁边时，我们都很高兴。

一个寒冷的早晨，我醒来时听见妈妈在哭。"怎么了？"我跌跌撞撞地跑进厨房问道。爸爸默默地坐在桌旁，妈妈转过头来看着我，她的脸上满是泪水。"八公昨天晚上在涩谷火车站去世了，"她哽咽着说道，"直到死，它还在等上野博士。"

那年我已经 17 岁了，不能随便掉眼泪了。但我走进另一个房间，很长时间都没有出来。

那天晚些时候，我们去了火车站。让我们大为吃惊的是，报摊旁边八公每天等待的地方摆满了它的朋友们送来的鲜花。

小林老先生也来了。他步履蹒跚地走到我身旁，一只手搭在我肩上。

"八公昨晚没有回家，"他平静地说道，"我走到火车站，找到了它。我觉得它的灵魂现在和上野博士的灵魂在一起，你觉得呢？"

"我想是的。"我轻声道。

　　八公巨大的铜像成了人们约会见面的一个胜地。现在的涩谷火车站很大，每天有成千上万的人往来于此。人们总是互相约定："我们在八公见吧。"今天，八公成为久未见面的朋友和家人再次相聚的地方。

背后的故事

几年前，我们一家搬到了东京，在离涩谷火车站不远的地方租了一套房子。那里的每个人似乎都知道在那个巨大的火车站约见面要约在八公雕像前。无论白天还是晚上，我去涩谷火车站时，总能看到有人站在那只大铜狗旁，眼睛在人群中搜寻。

我的日本朋友向我讲述了八公的故事。八公于1923年11月出生在日本北部，几个月后，它被送给了东京的上野博士。当上野博士于1925年5月21日去世时，他们才在一起生活了一年多。

1932年10月，一名报社记者发表了一篇关于八公的报道。这篇文章的标题是《忠犬守望七年，只为等待亡主归来》。日本各地的人们开始造访涩谷，只为看一眼忠犬八公。

  八公在涩谷火车站等待了近 10 年。它于 1935 年 3 月 7 日去世。在它去世的前一年，八公的铜像就已经在涩谷火车站入口附近落成，就在它每次等待上野博士的地方旁边。铜像旁边有一张真实的八公的老照片，照片中一群人簇拥在八公周围，而八公似乎在想，这些人围着我干什么。

在第二次世界大战期间，日本军队极度缺乏金属，包括八公雕像在内的许多雕像都被熔化了。但八公并没有被遗忘。1947 年，在第二次世界大战已经结束几年后，原八公雕像的雕塑家之子为八公雕刻了一座新雕像。这座雕像至今仍一动不动地守在涩谷火车站。

每年春天，涩谷火车站都会举行特别仪式，庆祝八公节。庆祝活动在每年的 4 月 8 日举行，也就是八公忌日的一个月后，这时的东京樱花盛放。涩谷区区长、警察局局长和车站站长都会参加庆祝活动，一名神道教祠官负责主持仪式，八公的朋友们则纷纷前来欣赏摆放在雕像周围的美丽花环。

我觉得八公的故事很美好，既悲伤又美好，我想把它分享给人家。健太郎是为这个故事而虚构的人物，但我相信，住在涩谷火车站附近的许多孩子不仅知道八公，还很喜欢它。

Hachiko

There is a statue of my old friend at the entrance to Shibuya Station. His bronze feet are bright and shiny, polished by thousands of friendly hands. There is a sign that says, simply, "Loyal dog Hachiko." I close my eyes and remember the day we met, so long ago.

When I was six years old, my family moved to a little house in Tokyo near the Shibuya train station. At first the trains frightened me. But after a while, I grew to enjoy their power and the furious noises they made. One day I begged Mama to take me to meet Papa as he came home on the afternoon train. She laughed and said, "Kentaro, you have become big and brave, just like a samurai!" Together we walked to the station.

It was spring, and the day was clear and cold. There were tiny carts all around the station, selling snacks, newspapers, and hundreds of other things to the crowds of people rushing by. Ladies in kimonos walked carefully, trying to keep their white tabi socks away from the grime of the streets. Businessmen strode about, hurrying home or to catch another train. Mama and I had stopped near the station entrance when I noticed the dog.

He was sitting quietly, all alone, by a newspaper stand. He had thick, cream-colored fur, small pointed ears, and a broad, bushy tail that curved up over his back. I wondered if the dog was a stray, but he was wearing a nice leather harness and looked healthy and strong.

His brown eyes were fixed on the station entrance.

Just then, Papa appeared. He was chatting with an older man. The dog bounded over to the man, his entire body wiggling and quivering with delight. His eyes shone, and his mouth curled up into something that looked, to me, just like a smile.

"Ah, Kentaro! You see, Dr. Ueno, you are not the only one who has someone to welcome him," said Papa. He introduced us to the older man. "Dr. Ueno works with me at Tokyo Imperial University."

"What is your dog's name?" I asked timidly. The dog was beautiful, but his sharp face reminded me of a wolf's. I grabbed Mama's kimono and stepped behind her, just in case.

"Don't be afraid," said Dr. Ueno kindly. "This is Hachiko. He is big, but still a puppy. He walks me to the station every morning and waits for me to come home every afternoon. I think Hachiko stores up all his joy, all day long, and then lets it out all at once!"

Hachiko stood wagging his tail next to Dr. Ueno. I reached out to touch him, and he bounced forward and sniffed my face. I yelped and jumped back behind Mama.

They all laughed. "Oh, Kentaro, don't worry—he just wants to get to know you," said Dr. Ueno. "Dogs can tell a lot about people just by smelling them. Why, Hachiko probably knows what you ate for lunch!"

I sniffed my hand, but it didn't smell like rice balls to me. I reached out and touched Hachiko gently on the

shoulder. "His fur is so thick and soft," I said. "Like a bear's."

"Dogs like Hachiko once hunted bears in the north, where it is very cold and snowy," said Dr. Ueno, kneeling down next to me and rubbing Hachiko's ears.

From that day on, I went to the station almost every afternoon. But I no longer went to see the trains. I went to see Hachiko. He was always there, waiting near the newspaper stand. I often saved a morsel from my lunch and hid it in one of my pockets. Hachiko would sniff me all over, wagging his tail, until he found a sticky bit of fish or soybean cake. Then he would nudge me with his nose, as if to say, "Give me my prize!" When it was cold, I would bury my face in the thick ruff of creamy fur around his neck.

One day in May, I was waiting at the station with Hachiko. The moment I saw Papa, I knew something was wrong. He was alone, and he walked hunched over, staring sadly at the gray pavement under his feet.

"What's the matter, Papa?" I asked him anxiously, standing with one hand on Hachiko's broad head. He sighed. "Kentaro, let's go home." Hachiko's bright brown eyes followed us as we walked away, but he stayed behind, waiting for Dr. Ueno.

When we got home, Papa told us that Dr. Ueno had died that morning at the university. I was stunned. "But what will happen to Hachiko?" I asked, blinking hard to keep the tears back. "What will he do?"

"I don't know," said Papa. "Perhaps Dr. Ueno's relatives will take him in."

"What about tonight?" I asked. "Can we go see if he is

all right?"

Papa was very sad and tired, but he walked with me back to Shibuya Station. Hachiko was curled up by the newspaper stand. He wagged his tail when he saw us. Papa and I gave him water in an old chipped bowl and some food. Hachiko ate and drank, but he kept looking up toward the station entrance for Dr. Ueno. Papa and I left even sadder than we had come.

The next day, I went back to check on Hachiko, but he was not there. Papa told me that Hachiko had been taken several miles away to live with some of Dr. Ueno's relatives. "But I'll never see him again!" I cried. "Why can't he live with us?"

"We don't have room for a dog," protested Papa. "And Hachiko really belongs to Dr. Ueno's relatives, now that Dr. Ueno is dead. Hachiko is better off having a home than sitting at a train station."

But Hachiko had other ideas. A few days later he was back at Shibuya Station, patiently waiting, his brown eyes fixed on the entrance. Hachiko had run back to his old home, and from there to Shibuya Station.

Mama and Papa let me take food and water to Hachiko every day. Mama grumbled a bit about the food, saying we couldn't afford to feed a big bear like Hachiko, but she always seemed to cook more rice than we could eat.

Other people at the station took an interest in Hachiko. Men and women who rode Papa and Dr. Ueno's train stopped by to scratch his ears and say a few kind words. One day I saw an old man filling Hachiko's water bowl as Hachiko licked his hand. The old man's hair was streaked with gray, and he was stooped, as if he had spent most of his life bent over the ground. But his eyes were as sharp and bright as Hachiko's.

"Are you young Kentaro?" the old man asked. I nodded.

"I'm Mr. Kobayashi. I was Dr. Ueno's gardener.

"Dr. Ueno told me that you and Hachiko often wait for the afternoon train together."

"Do you still take care of the house where Dr. Ueno lived?" I asked.

"Yes," said Mr. Kobayashi. "Hachiko comes back to the house every night to sleep on the porch. But in the morning, he walks to the station just like he did with Dr. Ueno. When the last train leaves the station, he returns home."

We were both silent. Then I asked, "Do you think Hachiko knows that Dr. Ueno died?"

Mr. Kobayashi said thoughtfully, "I don't know, Kentaro. Perhaps he still hopes that Dr. Ueno will return someday. Or perhaps he knows Dr. Ueno is dead, but he waits at the station to honor his master's memory."

As the years passed and Hachiko got older, he became very stiff and could barely walk to Shibuya Station. But still he went, every day. People began collecting money to build a statue of Hachiko at the station. Papa, Mama, and I all gave money, and we were very happy when the statue was placed next to the spot Hachiko had waited for so many years.

One chilly morning I woke to the sound of Mama crying. "What's wrong?" I asked as I stumbled into the kitchen. Papa sat silently at the table, and Mama turned her tear-stained face to me. "Hachiko died last night at Shibuya Station," she choked. "Still waiting for Dr. Ueno."

I was seventeen, and too big to cry. But I went into the other room and did not come out for a long time.

Later that day we all went to the station. To our great surprise, Hachiko's spot near the newspaper stand was covered in flowers placed there by his many friends.

Old Mr. Kobayashi was there. He shuffled over to me and put a hand on my shoulder.

"Hachiko didn't come back to the house last night," he said quietly. "I walked to the station and found him. I think his spirit is with Dr. Ueno's, don't you?"

"Yes," I whispered.

The big bronze statue of Hachiko is a very famous meeting place. Shibuya Station is enormous now, and hundreds of thousands of people travel through it every day. People always say to each other, "Let's meet at Hachiko." Today Hachiko is a place where friends and family long separated come together again.

The Story Behind the Story

Some years ago, my family moved to Tokyo, and we rented a home not far from Shibuya Station. Everyone, it seemed, knew that Hachiko's statue was the place to meet at the huge train station. No matter what time of day or night I visited Shibuya, I would always see someone standing near the large bronze dog, with eyes searching the crowd.

My Japanese friends told me Hachiko's story. Hachiko was born in northern Japan in November 1923, and a few months later he was sent to Dr. Ueno in Tokyo. When Dr. Ueno died on May 21, 1925, they had been together for just over a year.

In October 1932, a newspaper reporter wrote a story about Hachiko. The headline read: "A Faithful Dog Awaits the Return of Master Dead for Seven Years." People began traveling to Shibuya from all over Japan, just to pet loyal Hachiko.

Hachiko's vigil at Shibuya Station lasted almost ten years. He died March 7, 1935. One year earlier, a bronze statue of Hachiko had been placed near the entrance to Shibuya Station, right next to the spot where he always waited for Dr. Ueno. There is an old photo of the real Hachiko next to the bronze one, surrounded by a crowd of people. Hachiko seems to be wondering what all the fuss is about.

During World War II, the Japanese military was desperately short of metals. Many statues, including Hachiko's, were melted down. But Hachiko was not forgotten. In 1947, a few years after the war ended, the son of the original sculptor made a new statue of Hachiko. It stands there still.

Every spring, there is a special Hachiko festival at Shibuya Station. It is always held on April 8, one month after Hachiko's death anniversary, when Tokyo's cherry trees are in full bloom. The Shibuya mayor, police chief, and stationmaster are always there. A Shinto priest performs a ceremony, and Hachiko's friends come to admire the beautiful wreaths of flowers that are displayed around his statue.

I thought Hachiko's story was lovely, both sad and wonderful, and I wanted to share it. Kentaro was invented for this story, but I am sure many children who lived near Shibuya Station knew and loved Hachiko.

在此记录下你的感受，或写下属于你自己的"八公故事"。

八公教会了我忠诚的含义：

永远不应该忘记你爱过的每一个人。